SIEGE IN WINTER:

THE LANCASTRIAN SURRENDER

By J.P. REEDMAN

A WARS OF THE ROSES SHORT STORY

Cover-J.P.Reedman
Copyright Jan. 2024/J.P. REEDMAN/HERNE'S CAVE

King Edward, fourth of that name, had a nasty case of the measles.

His malady had begun with a cough—merely a common winter ague, the young Yorkist king had claimed as he led his army north to the city of Durham. Unfortunately, almost as soon as he arrived, this ague had progressed to a high fever that left him sweating and nigh delirious. Worst of all was when a splotchy red rash broke out across his torso, and then his infamously handsome face. The King's physics were called to his bedchamber and sadly proclaimed the worst—"You have *morbilli*, your Grace, also known as 'meazils.' It is a disease found most often in children, but on occasions a grown man can contract this malady too."

"Jesu!" Edward groaned, lying on the bed in his lodgings at the Bishop's Castle, which stood near the great Benedictine priory of Christ, the Virgin, and St Cuthbert. "What can I expect of these 'meazils'? Will I be marred for life?" He glared into a small polished bronze mirror held up by a quivering page. The King's image blurred and bulged on the not terribly clear surface. "I look like a bloody monster! My eyes are red, my nose running, and these things on my skin…They're not buboes, are they? Plague?"

"No, no, your Grace. Nought like buboes, I can assure you," said Doctor William Hobbys, chief among Edward's gaggle of physicians.

Edward growled and then went into a fit of coughing. "You still haven't answered my first question. Will I be disfigured by this…this pox?"

The physician licked his lips nervously. "It is not usually the case, sire. It is not the more deadly and disfiguring Variola."

Edward slumped back against the bolster, clearly relieved. "Well, thank God Almighty for that small mercy! So…when can I return to my royal duties?"

Hobbys began to tremble a little; Edward was a true Plantagenet and could be volatile when he heard things he did not wish to hear. "Your Grace, although it is not as lethal as Variola, measles is still a serious illness that takes the lives of many children or makes them deaf or blind."

Edward stared at Hobbys with his red, sore eyes, which gave him a most disconcerting appearance. "And? I am not a child. I am a man strong of limb and healthy…"

William Hobbys knotted his raw-boned hands together nervously and cleared his throat. "Your Grace, the problem is—it seems from my studies, and that of other doctors, that when a grown man or woman contracts measles, the disease is often more severe than in children. Not only does it carry the risk of blindness and deafness, it can affect the lungs…and sometimes even, on rare occasions…" He bowed his head, unable to meet the monarch's bloodshot eyes.

"You are saying I *could* die from this malady?" Edward sat up, his voice coming out like the roar of an angry lion. "After you implied it was almost harmless?"

"It is not unheard of, highness, I am sorry to report." Hobbys stared down at his feet miserably. It was never good fortune to give potential bad news to a king…

"But surely it is only the old greybeards or the sickly who succumb!" Edward cried. "Are you calling me weak, Hobbys? Answer me!"

"No—no, of course not, sire. But…to facilitate a full recovery, you must rest, and we must darken the chamber so that no harm will come to your eyes." The physician turned to his three fellows, standing in a line on the far side of the chamber, nodding wisely as they pretended to discuss the King's affliction. "Go find enough thick cloth to completely furl these windows." He gestured to the high, narrow windows on the eastern side of the bedchamber.

"I cannot rest! This is madness!" cried Edward, thumping the bed with one fist like an angry child having a tantrum. "I have an army to lead! The Lancastrian threat to my reign has not subsided. Margaret of Anjou lies in wait like a viper, watching for any weakness."

"You have many great captains, sire," said Hobbys, trying to soothe the King. "Surely one of them can lead—temporarily—in your place."

"But none are greater in the field than I!" Edward shouted, and in a fit of true Plantagenet temper, he grabbed a goblet from a stand at the bedside and hurled it with full force at the wall. It struck the stonework and bounced off, showering wine. The cup hit the ground with a clang and rolled, tracking red droplets. It had been a good quality cup with cabochons of many colours set round the rim. And it had belonged to the Bishop. Now it was dented, the stones popped from their settings.

Doctors, squires, and frightened pages stared at the wreckage. Edward gave a loud groan and clutched his temples. "Tell the Bishop I've wrecked his damned cup, but I'll replace it when I can," he ordered a squire, the same one that had earlier held the mirror so that the King could see his spotty face. The youth bowed and ran, relief written on his features. The other squires began to clean up the mess made by the King's thrown goblet.

"There must be some curatives I can take to at least shorten the course of this illness," said Edward, looking rather desperate now.

"We could bleed you, your Grace," said William Hobbys dubiously. "Remove bad humours…"

"No…NO!" cried the young King, pounding the bed again with his hand. "I've seen strong men given that treatment who weakened and died! Just…*NO!*"

"We can have a drink brewed from coriander if any is available. That may help bring down your fever."

"That is *ALL* you can do?" Edward's expression was wild.

"I am afraid so, Highness. The illness must run its course."

"This is nonsense! I do not need your potions and cures!" Edward raged, pulling himself off the bed and striding towards the chamber door.

And then he faltered, his steps growing slow and doddering. His face blanched, and he clutched his chest as he was racked by a harsh, barking cough. "Attend to his Grace!" ordered Hobbys in alarm, and two squires raced to the King's side and supported him before he toppled to the floor. Carefully, they guided him back to the safety of the bed.

"My head…" groaned Edward, placing one hand on his brow. "It pounds like a drum! And…the whole world is spinning…"

"As I said," Doctor Hobbys admonished, leaning over him, growing more confident, now that he had been proved correct in his assessment of the seriousness of the King's condition. "You must rest in Durham and let others go to war."

"Get the Earl of Warwick!" grunted Edward. "And get me that coriander tisane—I am burning up as if a fire is lit beneath my skin."

The physician nodded and called out to his compatriots. "You, Hattecliffe, get the king a draught for his fever…and something to put on the lesions. The rest of you—why are those hangings not yet over the windows as I asked? Do it…*NOW*!"

There was much rustling as doctors and squires rushed about the bedchamber, busy as ants.

The room fell into darkness.

Edward lay on the bed in the darkened chamber, a damp cloth laid over his eyes. A solitary candle burned. The physics shuffled around, carrying potions, jars of hot unguents, and wet towels used to bring the King's fever down.

Richard Neville, Earl of Warwick, stood in the doorway, not sure if he should enter.

William Hobbys raised his head and glanced in his direction. "Have you had *morbilli* before, my Lord Earl? The measles?"

The Earl, a tall and rugged man of great character and daring, looked uncharacteristically alarmed at this question. "What …what is it you ask, Hobbys? Why do you need to know such a thing?"

The doctor's expression became peevish at Warwick's reticence. "I need to know so I might judge as to whether it is safe for you to enter his Grace's chamber. In my studies, it has been noted that if one has contracted measles in the past, it is exceedingly rare for the disease to ever return, even if you are in direct contact with one afflicted."

Warwick folded his arms, deep in thought. "Aye, I believe I had this malady when I was a small child. It spread about the nursery and ran amok in the nearby villages too."

The physician nodded. "If that is true, you may then safely enter."

Neville stepped over the threshold and approached the large figure slumped under a coverlet on the bed. "Edward…your Grace?" he asked cautiously. "Are you awake?"

"Of course I am awake, Dick," mumbled Edward, sounding very out of sorts. Weakly, he propped himself up on one elbow. A cloth was tied around his head, covering his sensitive eyes.

"How do you feel?"

"Sicker than I've ever been in my life!" replied the King through gritted teeth.

Warwick was silent for a moment, then he said slowly, "And what is your wish, your Grace?"

"What do you think, Dick? To be well again! To lead the army as I am accustomed, giving my men heart and courage against my enemies. As it is, Hobbys says I may be in bed at least a week, perhaps two. By the time I am hale again, it may be too late." He pulled himself completely upright, swinging his legs over the side of the bed so that he faced Richard Neville at a less indecorous angle. "I am going to ask you to fare deep into Northumberland in my stead. We cannot let the castles of Bamburgh and

Dunstanburgh remain in Lancastrian hands."

Warwick shook his head. "Ralph Percy has been Constable at Dunstanburgh and Bamburgh for years. He refused to leave even when Queen Margaret's forces retreated and fled back to Scotland. The Duke of Somerset, Henry Beaufort, is also dwelling at Bamburgh; he heard it was impregnable, so he stayed."

"Both castles are Lancastrian-infested nests. I need you to clear out those rat's nests. How do you fare with the Percy stronghold of Alnwick?"

Warwick smiled thinly. "I am sure I can take the seaward castles, your Grace. Indeed, I look forward to this enterprise. I shall continue to hammer on Alnwick's gates, too, although that fortress may be a harder nut to crack. But if Henry Beaufort and Ralph Percy are holed-up rats—I shall be the cat who plays with them ere they are devoured."

"Be my cat then, Dick," said Edward. He pulled the cloth from his face; beneath, his eyes were still red and oozing.

Warwick fought the natural urge to step back at the sight of those inflamed eyes. "I will, your Grace." He gave a quick bow. "I will ride to Warkworth at tomorrow's dawn and devise the ruin of these Lancastrian strongholds."

"Good." Edward placed the cloth over his sore eyes once more, a page tying it tightly so that it would not slip. Edward groped about, blind, crawling back into bed. "Doctor Hobbys!" he shouted. "Find me some potion that will soothe my aching head!"

Mist rolled in from the sea, covering Dunstanburgh Castle. A fairly new castle, as it was accounted, Thomas, Earl of Lancaster, had built it in the early 1300s. With the nearest villages across long grassy fields at Craster and Embleton, it was a remote and lonely fortress, where the walls shuddered and vibrated as the grey waves smote their fists against the cliffs it stood upon. The keep was almost always cold, with wind whistling through chinks in the stonework, while the curtain wall and the interior buildings needed constant repair, not only from the constant crash of the sea but also from the lash of rain, snow, wind, and sea-salt.

Ralph Percy strode along the battlements of the mighty donjon, which was the original gateway into the castle but was now the 'lord's tower,' while a newer gate with a barbican gave access to the inner wards instead. It was freezing, the wind howling out of the north, so he wore layers of heavy furs against the chill, making him appear a brawny giant, a bear. He squinted into the murk, staring this way and that over the nearby countryside, looking for anything untoward—not that he could see much in the enfolding mist.

Melancholy gripped Ralph's heart. He had ever been loyal to King Henry and Queen Margaret, so he had swiftly reverted to their cause rather than support Edward of York, whom he had sworn to, under duress, only a few months back. He had been overjoyed when Margaret finally reached Bamburgh with an army of French mercenaries near the beginning of November, but the joy felt at their arrival was short-lived. On hearing of the Earl of Warwick and Edward's massive armies streaming up to the north, the Queen's army began to waver without a single blow being struck. They tried to retreat to *Insula Sacra*, the Holy Isle, but a sudden storm struck, impeding their departure. Four hundred soldiers were captured or slain on the isle, many by a Yorkist known as the 'Bastard Ogle'—Ogre, more like. Thank God Almighty, the stalwart Margaret escaped in a fishing boat, accompanied by her loyal French commander, Pierre de Breze, and reached Berwick unharmed.

But Ralph had not departed with the Queen's men. Northumberland was his home, and he was a Percy, brother of the earl. It was his duty to stay here and hold the two castles till the Queen regrouped her forces and tried to invade again. Still, it was a lonely life out on the coast with the eerie sea-fog, endless screaming of gulls, and the roaring, crashing tides. His second wife, Jane, and his youngest daughter, Catherine, were far away at one of his inland manors, away from all these disputed castles, while his six children from his first wife Eleanor were spread about the households of noblemen.

He drew his furs more tightly around his bulky frame as he continued his slow march along the icy wall. Gulls screeched above, soaring on the stiff winds, their cries high and plaintive, as mournful as the wails of lost souls. The sea was particularly wild today, the sound of pebbles rolling in the tides like the sound of the demons' teeth gnashing in Hell.

The thought of lost souls and Hell was not a pleasant one. Ralph began to think of poor old Thomas of Lancaster, who had railed against Edward II's favourites, Piers Gaveston, after Piers had rudely nicknamed Thomas 'the Fiddler'. He loathed the social-climbing

Despensers too. After his rebellion at Boroughbridge failed, he attempted to flee to remote Dunstanburgh—but ended up on the block at his own castle of Pontefract. Some said his ghost was here at Dunstanburgh, a pale wraith in the frequent sea-fogs, who tottered around the walls on skeletal feet, his hollow eye-holes filled with bale-fire, his skin yellow and shrunken as parchment, and the thin wisps of his hair stolen by the resident gulls to feather their nests. He would wail at the gate, begging for admittance, his grinning teeth a-chatter in his bare skull.

Sir Ralph had never seen this foul spirit, though, and doubted he ever would. "A story for simpletons," he murmured to himself. "Too much drink or too much imagination."

He shuffled toward the sentry on duty, sitting beside a small fire brazier and looking half-frozen, his bow lying at his feet.

He felt a small frisson of pity for the man, stuck here through what would no doubt prove to be a lacklustre Christmas. No feasting here, nor anywhere within the area marked for attack by Edward of York.

"You—your name is Giles, isn't it?"

"Yes, sir." The man jolted upright, surprised at being spoken to by the castle's Governor. "Giles Pauncefoot."

"A foul night."

"It is that, sir, but at least it's not snowing or blowing a nor'easter. That would be far worse than a bit of mist."

"At least snow or storms might keep our foes away…" Percy mumbled, staring off into the murk over the sea.

Pauncefoot grunted. "You think they'll come then?"

Ralph shrugged. "It is in God's hands. I heard a rumour York is ill…may it be serious!"

Pauncefoot hawked and spat over the parapet. "That's what I think o' York's get. May his illness kill him off."

Ralph Percy sighed, his breath fogging around his stubbled lips. He felt grimy and uncouth, the barber not having shaved him in a week—but there was no time for such niceties. As soon as Margaret's army had fled, Ralph had thrown everything into preparing Dunstanburgh for a potential attack. He had corresponded with Henry Beaufort at Bamburgh, who had agreed to do the same—although he had no doubt young, hot-headed Henry would not exactly go without on Christmas Day, even if a full-blown banquet was out of the question. He was a Duke, and made sure everyone knew of his high status.

Darkly, Ralph thought of the stores in Dunstanburgh's larder; he had checked the supplies himself, and there wasn't much there, a barrel of smoked fish, some salted meat, dried-out vegetables, a few tuns of ale. He had sent to Craster and Embleton to makes purchases, but the harvest had been poor that year, and there was little on offer. He wondered if Henry had found the same at Bamburgh, but the younger man was poor at answering the letters Percy sent down the coast by courier.

He went to the crenels, stared out. The grass before the castle walls was frozen white, glittering faintly, but the fog was lifting. Dawn was near; on the horizon, the mist turned a vivid pink.

And then in the distance, he spied a movement, a flurry of shapes in the thinning haziness. He leant forward, straining his eyes. The wind was behind him, bearing down from the north. It was carrying any sounds away on its boreal breath.

Just shadows and mist. Night fog and imagination…

Suddenly the gale dropped to almost nought—a vague hissing across the nearby fields. A cloud tore apart in the east and wan sunlight filtered through the parting threads and burnt away the mist in its path.

The burgeoning light twinkled on something still partly hidden in the dissipating fogbanks. A spear. A sword. A helmet.

Ralph Percy clutched the crenels with his gloved hands. "They come!" he cried, making Pauncefoot jump to attention, his bow in his hand. "The enemy has come, like thieves in the night."

Richard Neville, the Earl of Warwick, sat on his mount viewing the great castle that loomed ghost-like through the sea-fog. He realised his army had been spotted, for he could see fires blossoming to life atop the battlements even as he watched.

He leaned forward on his saddle, appraising its defences. Dunstanburgh was a fine castle in appearance, but perhaps a little inferior in its construction, just as Warkworth had been. That castle had fallen easily and had proved a useful base for his operations in Northumberland. Warkworth was a rather pleasant acquisition, he thought, with a tight smile. A castle of unusual design, built more for pleasure than war, set in a bend of the River Coquet. From the top of the tall centremost tower, one could survey the lie of the land for miles around…

Dunstanburgh was more martial in appearance, forbidding in its remoteness and in the way it hugged high, bird-haunted cliffs, but it had neither the thickness of masonry nor the height of the walls of Bamburgh and Alnwick, the other mighty fortresses of the north.

John Tiptoft, the Earl of Worcester, bare-headed and clad in black armour, rode up to Warwick's side on his destrier. Tiptoft's first wife had been Warwick's sister, Cecily, and his star was on the rise under Edward IV, having recently been granted the position of Constable of the Tower. "My Lord Earl, what plans? Shall we commence building a siege tower? Or should we get a ram prepared to smite the gates?"

Warwick rubbed his chin thoughtfully. "It would be a shame, do you not think, to wreck this handsome castle?"

Tiptoft stared ahead at Dunstanburgh; he had cold, piercing eyes in a pale, oval face. "My Lord Warwick?"

"I am sure the King would prefer this fine building to remain as intact as possible—it might prove useful to him in the future, and he might want to enjoy it, should he soon be well enough to journey here. I wish to parley with the castle's governor before any hostilities proceed."

Warwick dismounted and strode to his newly set up tent, calling a herald into his presence. Soon the herald, his tabard a splash of vivid colour, was galloping through mist aflame with sunrise towards the mighty, pronged towers of Dunstanburgh.

The meeting was set for noon in the middle of the field. Warwick came forward alone to meet with Ralph Percy, while a row of bowmen and pikemen lingered several paces behind him. Percy had also come almost unaccompanied. Two soldiers, craggy-faced and grizzled as the sea-beaten castle walls, stood uncomfortably on the frozen grass.

Neither side expected any violence between the Earl and Ralph Percy at this meeting; such a thing was frowned upon when engaged in parlay, even in those turbulent times.

Percy looked haggard, his hair in disarray, bags under his eyes; his demeanour was glum. Warwick, however, appeared well-refreshed and of good cheer. He greeted Percy in an almost friendly fashion, rather than as an aggressive enemy. "It pains me to have to visit you in these circumstances, kinsman," he said.

Percy hardly knew what to reply to that. They were indeed kin; cousins, in fact. His mother, Eleanor Neville, was the sister of Warwick's father, Richard, who had been beheaded after the Battle of Wakefield. This also made Ralph a cousin of Edward of York, whose mother Cecily was Eleanor's younger sister. Edward, whom Ralph considered a usurper and a traitor to his rightful king. Edward—whom he had sworn to serve when he had little free choice, quickly reverting to his Lancastrian loyalties. He was aware of York's reputation for both valour and ruthlessness in war; he recalled the recent carnage of Palm Sunday Field at Towton. Blood had swelled the river, dyeing it crimson; Edward had given no quarter. Heaps of slain men, some brutalised by having noses slit or ears hewn off, still lay where they fell, rotting, filling the nearby fields with gaseous emanations that glowed green at dusk and made superstitious men believe they had seen revenants…

Unwittingly Ralph raised his hand to his throat, as if protecting it from the bite of the headsman's axe. Edward had spared him once already and he had sworn an oath to him—he doubted he would spare him a second time. He tried to muster up the courage to laugh in Richard Neville's face, to say, "I may share your blood through a woman, but my father was a Percy who died at St Alban's because of you and those you now serve, and I am the grandson of the great Henry Hotspur…' But he restrained himself, remembering as he did the fate of his grandfather. Great he might have been, but it did not stop Hotspur from falling afoul of a King and having his body dragged from the grave, propped between two millstones, then quartered in a posthumous execution…

Warwick must have noticed his nervous gesture, for he suddenly smiled. "He will pardon you again," he said. "If you surrender. He truly does not want to spill more blood of good Englishmen. Come, you are not a foolish man. Henry is led by his French wife like a cow on a rope. He has brought little but disaster to the country—and because of his many ill-starred choices, he has now lost all the English properties in France. The old fellow needs to be put out to pasture somewhere…like a remote Benedictine monastery. He would no doubt be happier there."

Ralph cleared his throat, shifting uneasily from one foot to the other. "Even if King Henry abdicated—he has a son."

"Does he?" Warwick gave a subtle shrug. "Many think her Grace was a little too *friendly* with Edmund Beaufort. You must admit it was strange that no child was born to her before the eighth year of her marriage to Henry, and that Henry had to be given help…" he bit back a laugh…"to perform his marital duties!"

"I will not listen to such slander," mumbled Percy. "I came to discuss terms."

"I have told you already. Surrender now or my army will remain here until you decide to capitulate. If you make this siege protracted, I am not certain King Edward will still hold open the offer of pardon to you…or your men."

He glanced over Ralph Percy's shoulder towards the castle, now, in the grey, wintry daylight, a vast giant slumbering on the brow of the hill.

"Sometimes in this kind of warfare…a game is played. One life taken for every day a siege wastes. I wonder if it is a game King Edward would like to play? He enjoys games. How many men would you condemn to die by your stubbornness, Percy? Or how many lives would you spare, if you did the right thing and surrendered here and now?"

"You speak too freely!" Anger flooded through Ralph Percy in a hot red tide. "Yes, I swore an oath to Edward of York, but under duress—it meant nothing and cannot bind me. He is treacherous and a usurper. There will be no surrender. And I have nought more to say to you, my Lord of Warwick. *Kinsman*."

He whirled on his heel, turning his back on Warwick. He was all too aware of how many armed men were facing his back, many carrying longbows. One swift arrow between the shoulder blades was all it would take to finish him.

But he surmised Richard Neville would be more honourable than to see him felled from behind. He would have never have agreed to meet him if he had thought otherwise.

But one never truly knew what dwelt in men's hearts, not in the terrible strife between warring kings and cousins. Whole families had been torn apart and loyalties changed or forgotten…

Blood roaring in his ears, he trudged slowly back towards Dunstanburgh's gates, his two guards thudding stolidly beside him.

He reached it safely, the shadow of the massive gatehouse apartments falling over him, enfolding him. As he made for the entrance, he suddenly heard an ominous sound, a high-pitched whine like an angry bee.

"Jesu!" he cried, flinging himself onto his face in the mud.

An arrow struck a stone a good ten feet away, bouncing back and falling harmlessly to the ground.

It had never been meant to hit him.

It was a warning.

In the distance, carried on the freezing north wind, he heard the sound of the Earl of Warwick's archers, laughing uproariously.

Laughing at him.

Ralph Percy screamed a curse into that bitter wind.

Warwick returned to his encampment. His pavilion was as comfortable as could be expected in a field in the middle of nowhere that was near the raging North Sea. His squires divested him of his cloak and heavy outer layers, and he sat down to dine, beginning with a goblet of heated, spiced wine and then a platter of spiced fish. It was the beginning of Advent, so he should have foregone the wine—but there were always extenuating circumstances, and he was in no fear for his immortal soul…

Richard Neville feared but little.

A short while after he had finished his meal, his captains, Worcester, Sir Ralph Grey, and Lord Scrope, came to the tent to discuss what was to be done in regards to Dunstanburgh.

"The response was, as I expected, a firm 'no,' said Warwick, sipping on his wine. "Ralph Percy will not surrender, not yet anyway. He seemed to believe King Edward is lying about granting him a second pardon."

Worcester almost grinned at that but forced his face into solemnity.

Neville pretended not to notice. "My Lord Earl," asked Grey, earnestly, "what then is the plan of action? The Earl of Worcester spoke earlier about building a siege tower."

Warwick flung back his head and laughed, then beckoned to a squire for a refill of his goblet, the contents of which he flung back with gusto. "You are ever-eager to build that blessed Tower, aren't you, Worcester?" he jested. "My answer is no. A waste of resources and manpower. I am quite sure that all we have to do is wait. Before long, the castle's garrison will have no fuel and likely no food. Percy appeared half-starved already. The castle will surrender when that time comes."

Ralph Percy strode around his solar like a beast locked within a cage.

What was he to do for the best? He knew Dunstanburgh could not sustain a long siege, and he was quite certain the Earl of Warwick and his cronies knew it too. His squire trembled before him as he brought in his master's supper on a platter. Percy stared down into the mess of pottage, poking it angrily with his knife. Suddenly he began to shout furious oaths and flung the pewter dish against the wall. It clanged loudly as it fell to the floor, showering contents over the threadbare Turkey carpets and the worn tapestries of huntsmen and classical warriors.

"S-sir?" The squire's knees fairly knocked together with fear. "H-have I displeased you…"

"My anger has nought to do with you, Peter," said Percy, his rage dying as swift as it had come. Now he merely looked weary, beaten, older than his years. "It's the food. Look at it."

The youth ran over to the fallen platter and began cleaning up the mess. As he did, his face screwed up in utter revulsion. "I see it now—there are worms in here. Maggots! Forgive me for bringing you such rancid fare…"

Ralph Percy went over to the squire and set his hand upon his shoulder. "It's not your fault, Peter; you just brought what the cook gave you. I place no blame on him, either—he is old, his eyesight is poor, and tapers we have few. He did not mean to offend or poison me, of that I am sure. What upsets me most is that it means our winter store, meagre to begin with, is contaminated. Rotten. Damn the dampness in the cellars of this castle."

"What shall we do, sir?" asked the lad as he finished mopping up the strewn pottage.

"I must think," said Percy, pressing his hand against his brow.

"There is only one possibility that comes to me—but the way is dark."

It was a dead hour, past midnight but long before the first flush of dawn. No light. Sir Ralph Percy crept from a postern gate behind the bulk of Dunstanburgh Castle. The exit was high on the seaward cliff face and the winds were fierce, nearly tearing him from his precarious perch. Below, the tides roared; the smash of the waves sent foam tossing into the air, blue-tinged in the gloom. One wrong move, one fierce blast of wind, and he would fall from the cliffside into the sea, never to be seen again, his bones rolling with the tides for eternity.

Carefully, carefully, he moved downward, step after step on a path barely visible as such; narrow steps hewn into basalt by unknown hands generations ago. He had planned and prepared for this possibility for over a year, ever since Edward won at Towton—a means to escape if needed. He had not used it the first time Edward had taken the Northumbrian castles, for it was a dangerous way, and submission had seemed wisest—but this second time was different. He had little faith that York would forgive.

Reaching the bottom of the cliffs after an eternity of clambering, gripping, sliding, slipping, Ralph stood panting as the damp sands sucked at his boots. Fumbling under his cloak with battered, bruised hands, he yanked a strike-a-light from his belt-pouch. He held it in shaking fingers, glancing nervously around him. If he was spotted…all was doomed.

The light flared out, a small flame but bright; just as quickly as it shone out, he doused it.

And stared into the whirling darkness, waiting, heartbeat a loud drum in his ears.

And there it was, a brief returning flash amidst the murk and sea-foam. Relief flooded him, and he staggered across the beach with as much speed as he could manage. Beyond a fan of stone jutting out of the spray, he saw a humble little boat bobbing on the swell and the old fisherman from Craster who was in his pay.

"Good eventide, sir." The grizzled fisherman, grey-bearded, hair a straggling cloud, face shrivelled as a dry kipper, grinned toothlessly at Ralph Percy. He paddled the rowboat as close as possible to the shore. "Thought this night might never come—but I was always waitin' for your light. Glad you made it safe down yon cliff." He nodded his grizzled head in the direction of the postern gate.

"We must be off, or all will be in vain." Ralph dashed into the freezing water, gasping as the shock of it ran through his body, and quickly hauled himself into the boat, making it sway dangerously from side to side. "I do not know who may be watching us even now. Is it safe to set out in the current tides?"

The greybeard's grin widened. "Aye, sir, there's nought to worry about tonight. I been boating in these waters since I was a lad, never fear you. I know the scent of a storm; I know the drumbeats of the water. Tonight—a little swell, no more. You are safe in my hands, Sir Ralph; I swear it by the Virgin."

Ralph grunted, still not entirely convinced, but he settled himself into the little craft nonetheless. He had no other choice.

"Make for Bamburgh, and may the winds be at our backs, driving us there with all speed!"

Ralph Percy arrived at Bamburgh as the dawn began to break. Shafts of early sun turned the red sandstone castle into a vision of flame as he climbed from the rowboat and hurried toward the fortress. Still cautious, he glanced around him. The beach was empty, the silver sand flying in small whirlwinds over the grass-topped dunes. So, he had made it in time; Warwick's forces had not yet approached—although he knew it was only a matter of time. Now, if he could manage to save this castle, perhaps the siege at Dunstanburgh could also be relieved.

It was with disbelief that the sentries at the gate saw their castle Constable striding, alone, towards the twin towers of the barbican. "Just let me in, damn you!" he shouted as they hesitated, confused by this unexpected arrival. "I'm not a goddamned ghost, and I am wet and cold!"

Soon Ralph was in the solar being pacified by a quivering steward. He pushed the man away as he tried to solicitously drape a warm fur over Percy's sodden, salty raiment. "Do not worry about my well-being!" he snorted. "I have more important things to attend to than my own comfort! Where is the Duke of Somerset?"

"Still abed, Sir Ralph," trembled the steward, a timorous little man that Percy thought resembled a frightened rabbit, all big eyes and prominent teeth.

"Well, *get him…*"

"Oh, good Sir, I dare not." The steward stared at his feet, wringing his hands in distress. "I fear it would not go well for me. He is very…particular, about his rest. He seldom rises before Terce."

I fear I may knock out those rabbity teeth, thought Ralph Percy, uncharitably, but then he waved a dismissive hand at the cowering steward, and said, "Enough wittering, man. I shall go to him myself."

Percy thudded down the corridors towards the castle's apartments. When he reached the one allotted for high-ranking guests, he rapped heavily on the closed door with a clenched fist. "Your Grace, are you in there?"

For a moment there was no sound, then came the noise of a bedframe creaking, and a voice yelled, "It's barely light. Unless you've come to tell me that the world is ending…piss off!"

"That is close enough to what I have come to tell you," Ralph shouted back. "Do you not recognise my voice, Duke Henry? It is Sir Ralph Percy,

Constable of this castle." He shoved at the chamber door, and to his surprise found it unbarred.

He strode into the bedchamber, which was in a horrific state—clothes strewn hither and thither, a scared page and a squire cowering on pallets, blankets drawn up to their terrified eyes, and Henry Beaufort emerging from the bed, bleary-eyed, his hair a wild spray, his hose half undone, a wine-stained night shirt billowing around him. All around the room were signs of merry-making, Advent or no—platters with half-eaten goose, crumbs from sweetmeats, cheese rinds, and pasties gnawed to the crust. Several empty wine carafes sat on table, chest, and window ledge.

"Well, I see you haven't been denying yourself this Advent," said Ralph, regretting his words even as he spoke. Governor of Bamburgh he might be, but Henry Beaufort was a Duke and of royal ancestry—and behaved every bit as if he thought himself a prince. He also had a hot temper and was not a man one would like to cross.

Beaufort, however, did not seem to pay any heed to his words; he was more astounded by the sight of Percy, smelling of sea-salt and red-faced from the wind. "What are you doing here? I thought you were at Dunstanburgh?"

"I was, my Lord Duke," said Ralph between gritted teeth, "but I've run into a slight problem."

"Which is?" The Duke snapped his fingers at the page and squire, and they came running to him with fresh clothes, a comb for his snarled hair, a water basin where he could lave his face.

Percy felt like a pot about to boil over. Did Beaufort really not know? Or had he just grown too cocky? Forces under his command had been foremost amongst those who took down Richard, Duke of York, at Sandal Castle in the winter of 1460. That slightly unsavoury act—Henry had broken a Christmas truce to get at his foe—had only increased his popularity with Queen Margaret, who heaped favours on him as she had his father. However, many men regarded Henry's actions that day as excessive; Beaufort had dishonoured his fallen enemy's body before allowing Lord Clifford to murder, without censure, York's seventeen-year-old son, Edmund.

Now Henry Beaufort seemed not only to be suffering a sore head from too much drink—but also a swollen head from too much arrogance.

"You haven't answered me, Percy. Why on earth have you come crashing in here at such an ungodly hour?" Beaufort snatched a proffered towel from his squire and rubbed his damp face vigorously.

"You must have had some intelligence coming in from spies and scouts, your Grace," said Ralph curtly. *But did you pay attention—since you've got little intelligence in your pride-addled skull...* "The Earl of Warwick and his armies…"

"I know," interrupted Henry Beaufort. "He's squatting in Warkworth and has sent his minions, William Neville and Lord Scales, to assail the gates of Alnwick."

Ralph Percy glowered. "Do you think that is all he will attack? He is already at the gates of Dunstanburgh!"

"Ah, I see." Some of Henry Beaufort arrogance vanished. Percy was glad to see he looked a little paler.

"His army will be here soon, without a doubt. He has said as much.

They intend to take all of the castles back in one fell swoop."

"Shouldn't you have remained at Dunstanburgh, Percy?" Beaufort's ill temper began to resurface. "You've left the garrison on their own?"

Heat rose into Percy's cheeks, but he kept his tone level. "There is no food there, my Lord Duke. Supplies were scanty this year because crops throughout Northumberland were poor. What we have in the store has mostly been eaten…or the worms have got into it. Soon…the only meat left will be the horses."

Henry stared wide-eyed at that. "What…you say *what*?"

"If starving, the men will do it," said Ralph grimly.

"This is evil news," mumbled Henry, shaking his head. "What would you have me do?"

"On my way hither, in a little boat paddled by an ancient fisherman, I wracked my brain a thousand times to think how I might help the garrison of Dunstanburgh. I surmised I could requisition some of Bamburgh's stores—supplies were always easier to obtain here—and take them back. But how would I get them back into the castle? I considered mad things, like building my own trebuchet and hurling them over the walls—but that was but a foolish dream. A single man might slip out in the night, as I did, and come to the beach to collect his victuals, but many men and carts would be apprehended almost at once. So…I fear, despite my efforts, Dunstanburgh is on its own. May God have mercy on me for abandoning the castle to its fate, and may He also also have mercy on the souls of those who dwell within. But if I can render no aid there, perhaps I can be of some service at Bamburgh."

Henry Beaufort nodded. "I have numerous doughty knights in my entourage, and the garrison here is well-armed and well-trained, as you know."

"Yes, I do know," murmured Percy, "but at the moment, the strength of men is not what we need most. It is food and fuel. What are the supplies like in the larder? Can we hold out for long if a siege begins? I am certain it is Warwick's intention to besiege this castle as well as the other two."

"I…I am not certain," Beaufort said uneasily. He would not meet Ralph's gaze.

"Perhaps we should check them together, your Grace," said Percy. "Although perhaps I have nought to fear—there must be plenty, for it appears you have indulged yourself rather well since you arrived."

"I like not your tone!" Henry Beaufort bridled with rage, but Ralph ignored him; he had no time for a lordling's tantrums. Turning abruptly, he marched out of the chamber and strode down the corridor. The Duke of Somerset uttered an oath and sprinted after him.

The stores were almost as empty as those at Dunstanburgh. Some salted fish and several slabs of dried meat, a roll or two of pock-marked cheese, a crate of shrivelled vegetables, a keg or two of wine. There was evidence of poultry; scatters of feathers lay all over the floor. But there were no chicken carcasses to be found; presumably what was there had been devoured.

"You thought *this* would prove adequate for the garrison, my Lord

Duke?" Ralph held out his arms in a hopeless gesture.

"You are the Constable!" snapped Henry Beaufort, assuming a defensive stance.

"I cannot be in two places at once. *You* were left in charge here while I was at Dunstanburgh. If you felt you could not…*cope*…you should have been honest with me from the start, my Lord Duke. Perhaps you were not aware of the paucity of supplies? Never checked them? From the state of your chamber, it appears *you* never went without for a single day!"

"Your accusations are outrageous!" cried the young Duke, his colour high. "God's Teeth, what did you expect me to do? Magic the supplies in?"

"No. Merely to have a care for those men who defend the walls. The walls that keep *you* safe. Remember that

Warwick's father, Salisbury, was executed after the battle of Wakefield, and that York was his uncle. Richard Neville will want vengeance just as you wanted vengeance for your father. And Jesu, the young boy Clifford murdered…"

"I had nought to do with that, Percy!" cried Henry, hands curled into fists. "And Edmund of March was no innocent child—he wore armour and fought near his father."

"But he had, I am told, surrendered before he was killed. Clifford cared nothing for that. It was a dishonourable act, no matter what side you support in this war. And then to spike his head on Micklegate…" He glared at Beaufort.

"That was the Queen's doing!" insisted Beaufort. "It was what she wanted…"

"And look what such petty revenge has wrought," muttered Ralph, gesturing to the empty shelves, the pitiful provisions.

"You fret like an old woman," said Henry, defiant, dropping his pugnacious stance and folding his arms defensively instead. "Warwick's army may come to Bamburgh's beach…but I know something you do not."

"And are you going to enlighten me?"

"Two days ago, I received a missive saying that the Queen is preparing to march on Northumberland again, her own forces led by Philip de Breze and bolstered by Scots. They could arrive at any time."

"Could. Might. Maybe," Ralph said bitterly. "Do you think the Scots will keep to their promises?"

"They may well. It amuses me that you speak ill of them when you once relinquished the castles entrusted to you, knelt before the usurper Edward and swore loyalty—then promptly broke those oaths and handed them back to Queen Margaret."

"I did what was needed." Percy's eyes were black with anger. "I would have never held to my oath to Edward of York. I acted as I did so that the castles would not be slighted, not to save my own skin."

Beaufort shrugged. "Maybe you speak truly; I know not…but *I* am not going to worry overmuch. Margaret will not leave me to perish."

"So, it's 'Margaret' now, is it?" mocked Ralph. "Well, my Lord Duke, all I can say is this—I hope you enjoy eating horse. If this Scottish army vanishes like mist and Warwick is encamped without the walls, soon that is all we will have to dine upon. Unless you think we should dine upon each other."

He kicked one of the empty crates on the floor and stormed away into the bowels of Bamburgh's great keep, uncaring that he had turned his back on a man of much higher rank.

Henry Beaufort wanted to pursue him, to berate him for speaking so to his betters, but something held the younger man back. Mostly the fear that, Duke or no, he might find himself expelled from the castle gates—out into the shifting sand dunes where Richard Neville, Earl of Warwick, might soon be on the prowl.

It did not take long. Less than two days after Ralph Percy made his escape by sea from Dunstanburgh, Warwick arrived on Bamburgh beach with his brother, John Neville, Lord Montague, and Baron Robert Ogle, a former retainer of the slain Richard, Earl of Salisbury, and a Constable of the Bishopric of Durham—the Bishop there was yet another Neville. Masses of soldiers filled the sand dunes, erecting vast pavilions and tents.

Ralph and Henry Beaufort watched the approach of their enemies from a room high in the great keep. "I told you they would come," Percy murmured.

"The castle will hold," said Henry. "It must. It is known as one of the strongest in England."

"War is changing," shrugged Ralph. "Soon, with cannon fire battering stone, who knows what will happen? We had best hope Neville has not brought up any of his great guns, for I would rather not find out."

"Look—Warwick is coming to the gates," murmured Beaufort, suddenly gone a sickly green.

Sure enough, accompanied by a herald and his brother Montague, the Earl was approaching the gate astride a powerful destrier.

"Shall…shall I go to meet him?" asked Henry Beaufort, unenthusiastically. As the highest ranking, it was his duty, but he did not relish facing the man whose kin he slew without a sword in his hand.

Ralph shook his head grimly. "No, I am the Constable, here and at Dunstanburgh. I shall meet Warwick. I expect he will seek terms. Better for you, my Lord Duke, to keep out of sight—and hopefully out of mind. We do not want to incur Warwick's ire and make things worse for us. If he thinks to merely starve us out, rather than attack at once, there is always a chance that the Queen's Frenchman will show up with the Scottish mercenaries."

"They *will* come!" insisted Beaufort.

"Till then, there may be needs to tighten your belt, Lord Duke."

Ralph went down to the gatehouse and, alone, walked out onto the drawbridge before his foes.

Warwick stared at him in amazement and then released a burst of laughter. Montague and Ogle cast him surprised looks. "I did not expect this, Sir Ralph! Unless you have a twin brother or are a ghostly double-walker, or fetch, as they call such creatures on the Scottish border."

"No, I have no such brother, and I am very much of the mortal world," said Percy.

"How did this come to be? I am curious! I have some of my best men back at Dunstanburgh, and yet you clearly slipped away from under their very noses."

Ralph Percy flashed the Earl a crooked, joyless grin. "I am not going to divulge my secrets to a man such as you, my Lord Earl. I am not completely moon-mad."

"No, I suppose not." Warwick stroked his chin. "We'll leave such lunacy to the likes of your master, Old Henry. So, night flights aside, I must ask you again to surrender the castles."

"The answer is no, Lord Warwick," said Ralph firmly. "As it was at Dunstanburgh. No."

"Are you certain?" Warwick leaned forward over the plaited mane of his steed, fixing Percy with a long, hard gaze. "How long can these castles endure a siege?"

"Help is on its way." Ralph regretted his words even as they slid from his lips. He should not have told the Earl; there was always the chance he had not heard of Queen Margaret's latest attempt to bring an army into England.

But Richard Neville did not seem perturbed in the least. "You believe that, do you?

"I do," muttered Ralph, although, in truth, he had been dubious from the moment Henry Beaufort informed him.

"Then I think you will have a very long wait, Constable," said Warwick, and he drew upon his reins and galloped from Bamburgh's gates and back towards the enemy encampment, his departure blurred from Ralph Percy's vision by a veil of blowing silver sand...

It was the day before Christmas Eve, and the pantry in Bamburgh Castle was completely empty. Not even a crumb of cheese or wizened flake of fruit remained to tempt the mice that scuttled in the corners. The bakery ovens remained unlit, adding an extra chill to the great seaside fortress, and even the drink was all but gone, the remainder heavily mixed with water. The castle's well still seemed fine to use, but there were brave souls acting as tasters every night, in case Warwick had located the water source and poisoned it with animal carcasses. Snow began to fall heavily, sticking to the frowning face of the great rectangular keep and whitening the dunes below the ramparts. The sky brooded, promising further inclement weather. Out in the dunes, the enemy army sat patiently waiting, their fires dull orange blobs through the wintry murk.

Standing on the wall, Ralph Percy gazed out into the tumbling, wind-driven snowflakes. Faintly, ever so faintly, he made out Warwick's Bear and Ragged Staff banner. "How much strength does the man have?" he murmured. "Every day he comes here; it is said he journeys daily to each of the castles he has besieged, although the distance between all three is some seventeen leagues!"

He had to admit he grudgingly admired the Earl, enemy or no. He just wished Neville was still on the side of King Henry as he once had been long ago.

His thoughts were interrupted by the sound of footsteps. Glancing aside, he saw Henry Beaufort, wrapped in a rich fur-lined cloak, join him on the wall-walk. Within his drawn-up hood, the Duke's handsome face was pinched and pallid. "He is there again?"

"He is there!" Percy leaned on a crenel and frowned out like a gargoyle.

"There is no food—none at all now, I am told."

"Correct, my Lord Duke. We have reached the end…"

"The end," breathed Beaufort, his breath puffing before his chilled lips.

"The situation is desperate," murmured Ralph. "We still have water, but the nights are growing ever colder. If the water should completely freeze…" He shrugged. "The men are starving. They are weak, I can see the signs of privation in there faces. They fight with each other daily; their tempers grow short. Yesterday, I separated two of them who had attacked each other with knives. Over a stupid dice game! They had been friends before, now they loathe each other— lack of food turns decent men into beasts. Where will it go from there, think you? My Lord Duke, you and I may soon be the target of those knives."

"Margaret will come. She promised she would come." Henry Beaufort muttered the words like a prayer. "Look, I have not shown you before, but she gave me a token of her fidelity ere she fled—"

Ralph smelt the vague scent of liquor on the other man's breath as he leaned close; the Duke must have had some stashed away in his chamber. Beaufort pulled a flattened, withered red rose from within his doublet; it dangled pathetically from his fingers. Its one-time beauty forever lost.

"Promises, in these times, are as ephemeral as these snowflakes," said Ralph, catching a flake on his gloved hand and breathing upon it.

It melted instantly.

Henry Beaufort scowled and averted his eyes. One of the shrivelled petals on his gifted rose fell off and was borne away on the bitter wind.

Christmas Eve. The smell of roasting meat filled the halls of Bamburgh Castle. Advent was not yet over, not till the next day, but fasting had gone on long amidst the castle's garrison, and they had grown weak in both body and mind and desperate for sustenance. Prayers for forgiveness would come later; the Almighty would understand, and there was nothing some prayers and penance couldn't make right.

However, despite the rich aroma of cooking, the mood in the Great Hall of Bamburgh was sombre and uneasy. Faces were long, pallid, eyes underscored by dark stripes. The hall itself was dim, lit only by a nearly extinguished fire in the central hearth and the flickers of greasy, foul-smelling candles made from fat.

Henry Beaufort sat at the high table, stiff-backed, glassy-eyed. Ralph Percy sat next to him, slumped onto his bench, lips taut and white.

In came the servers, accompanied by a hushed silence. No trumpeters, no musicians, no tumblers or acrobats graced this Christmas feast.

The first platter was placed before Duke Henry, as befitting his station. Hot, meaty scents emanated from it; its warmth within the wintry chill of the hall made great clouds of steam rise upwards from it like ghostly fingers. The servers had covered the tray with a fine cloth, hiding the lumps and bumps of the food lying beneath.

Henry Beaufort stared at the platter as if frozen, making no gesture to command the two cowering servers to draw off the makeshift covering and reveal the festive meal.

"Are you not hungry for the feast, my Lord Duke?" asked Ralph, his voice scarcely above a whisper.

Beaufort made a noise as if he might gag.

"I will do the honours then," said Ralph, standing up and yanking the cloth away.

There on the platter lay a cooked horse's head in place of the traditional Christmas boar. Its big white teeth grinned horribly from amidst a sea of shrivelled winter vegetables.

"All we have left to eat are the horses," Ralph said quietly. "Unless you would prefer a scrawny dog or cat. But the garrison is rather fond of its pets—they might choose a different kind of meat, if you follow my thought."

Now Henry Beaufort *did* gag, pressing his napkin to his lips as his shoulders heaved. "Do-do not even jest so, you caitiff! We cannot…I cannot… A horse's head! Percy, this is *too* much! Abominable…"

"My Lord Duke." Ralph Percy bent low to whisper in the other man's ear. "The Queen is not coming. I think it is time…to call the surrender. We are done here. We cannot hold out any longer. It…is over."

Henry Beaufort gave a strangled cry of frustration, and taking his eating knife, plunged it into the horse meat on the platter. "Yes, then, *yes*. Do as you will!"

Choking and heaving, he rose, kicked over his seat in fury and stormed from the Great Hall.

Ralph Percy went to pray in the Chapel of St Peter. He was alone; above his head, falling snow rushed against the chapel roof. Near the high altar, the jewelled reliquary box containing the arm bone of St Oswald glittered in the chill darkness, its gems picked out by the solitary, sputtering taper.

He hoped he was doing the right thing—no, he *knew* he was. He and Beaufort might face the axe, despite Edward of York's supposed offer of further pardons—but capitulation would save the lives of the other men, ordinary men, who did not deserve to perish.

"If I am wrong, Lord, send me a sign," he murmured.

There was no sudden choir of angels, no shining light upon the Rood—but the little candle, caught by a draught, fluttered out, leaving the chapel in darkness.

That was the sign.
It was time to go.
Time to leave.
Time to surrender.

Ralph walked slowly down the slippery barbican into a white, snowbound world. The moon hung overhead, making the snow and frost blue and magical. Beside him walked one of the men-at-arms, holding up a large white flag.

Christmas Eve. Holy Eve.

Across the frozen landscape, Richard Neville, Earl of Warwick, came riding, the moonlight sliding off his armour. He reined in his mount before Ralph Percy. "I received your message, Sir Ralph. I see the white flag borne aloft by your man. What have you to say?"

Ralph gave a sigh. "My Lord Earl, upon this Christmas Eve, I, as Constable, formally surrender the castles of Bamburgh and Dunstanburgh to you." He reached out to his belt and took the huge keys he carried, more ceremonially than for general use, and handed them to the Earl.

"It is a wise decision," said the Earl. "The terms I spoke of before still stand. King Edward will be merciful."

Ralph Percy nodded. Words failed him now. He could say no more but, under escort, walked slowly towards the bright fires of Warwick's encampment.

And far, far away, perhaps in the little town that clustered near the foot of the mighty coastal castle, he heard a solitary voice raised in song, heralding the coming dawn and Christmas morn—

Of a Rose sing we:
Marvellous mystery!

This Rose is red of colour bright,
Through whom our joy came alight,

Upon a frosty Christmas night.
Of a rose sing we,
Marvellous mystery

A marvellous mystery indeed. The red rose of Lancaster was in decline, its petals falling like those of the flower Queen Margaret had given Henry Beaufort. Ralph Percy did not know what his future now held, but on that winter's eve, he was suddenly glad he had relinquished the castles to Warwick. No battle, no bloodshed.

It was Christmas.

Peace and good will to all men.

THE END

IF YOU HAVE ENJOYED THIS BOOK, PLEASE CHECK OUT MY OTHER WORKS ABOUT RICHARD III, THE WARS OF THE ROSES, LESSER-KNOWN MEDIEVAL QUEENS AND NOBLEWOMEN, STONEHENGE, ROBIN HOOD, AND BRITISH AND IRISH MYTH AND LEGEND

UK AMAZON LINK TO AUTHOR PAGE:
https://www.amazon.co.uk/J-P-Reedman/e/B009UTHBUE

USA AMAZON LINK TO AUTHOR PAGE:
https://www.amazon.com/stores/J.P.Reedman/author/B009UTHBUE

AUTHOR'S NOTE.
This short story is based on a real event. While leading his soldiers north,

Edward IV did indeed fall sick with measles and ended up bedridden in Durham, leaving Richard Neville, the Earl of Warwick, to take not one but three castles—Alnwick, Bamburgh and Dunstanburgh. Every day, Warwick did a round trip to visit all three and see how the sieges were going.

By Christmas Eve, the two coastal castles, Bamburgh and Dunstanburgh, were in trouble. All the food supplies were gone, and they garrison was reduced to eating their own horses. Sir Ralph Grey was the Constable of both castles, and on Christmas Eve he finally surrendered Bamburgh. Dunstanburgh surrendered a day or two later. (Alnwick lasted out a bit longer.)

I have played around a bit with Ralph Percy's movements during the sieges because I really wanted to include both castles, as they are two of my All-Time Favourites. Dunstanburgh, with its clifftop position and ruined gatehouse weathered into prongs like a giant crown, is extremely eerie and almost resembles a set from a fantasy film. Bamburgh is more complete, thanks to some restoration, and is beloved of many film and TV makers—it was Castle Belleme in HTV's Robin of Sherwood and was recently seen in The Last Kingdom and even in an Indiana Jones film!

Printed in Great Britain
by Amazon